RIKA *MECHANIZED*

RIKA'S MARAUDERS – PREQUEL

M. D. COOPER

Version 1.0.1

ISBN: 978-1-64365-005-0

Cover Art by Tek Tan
Editing by Jen McDonnell

TABLE OF CONTENTS

RIKA'S STORY & THE ORION WAR

If you've read any of the Orion War books, you'll know that the *Intrepid*'s arrival in the 90th century has shaken things up. One of those things is the long balance between the Genevian and Nietzschean empires.

Rika is just one woman who has been caught up in the growing conflict that is spreading across the Orion Arm of the galaxy. Things aren't going to be easy for her, but eventually she'll have a significant part to play on the larger stage.

HAMMERFALL

STELLAR DATE: 12.01.8941 (Adjusted Years)
LOCATION: Western plains of Naera
REGION: Parson System, Genevian Federation

"Alright, mech-meat, I want the three of you on that ridge to the south," Gunnery Sergeant Myers said as he pulled on his helmet. His voice changed from his surly growl to a voice in their minds as his armor closed up around him. <*You pick off any stragglers that come off their main column, and let me know if there's anything bigger than troop transports out there.*>

The three scout mechs saluted; the other two with their right hands, and Rika with her left.

Myers cocked his head, and she knew that if he weren't wearing a helmet, he would have spat. Maybe even on her. <*Fucking lefty.*>

Rika wished she could respond, swear at the gunnery sergeant; hell, she'd love to pound him into the dirt, and with the cybernetic limbs the Genevian military had given her, she could do it with ease.

If not for the compliance chip in her head. Even thinking about hitting the sergeant took her perilously close to a treatment of Discipline—excruciating pain that would tear through her body and drop her like a rock.

She glanced down at her right arm, its current configuration the cause of her left-handed salute. Where she once had possessed a flesh and blood limb, there was now just a rifle mount and ammunition feeder. The current weapon locked onto the mount was a twin-mode GNR-41B sniper rifle with a 120cm barrel. Not the ideal thing to attempt a salute with.

Her left arm, though it did not serve as a weapons mount, was also no longer hers, but the property of the Genevian military. Rika harbored no illusions on that front—*she* was the property of the Genevian military.

By some small miracle, the designers of the SMI-2, Scout-Mechanized Infantry—her model—had given her a real left arm. Not to say that it was a natural arm; her flesh and blood limb ended above the elbow there as well, but at least the cybernetic portion ended in a hand, robotic though it was.

When she first left the assembly plant, Rika had wondered why the military had replaced her left arm—until she felt the kick of an automatic rifle, and understood that the arm she had been born with could not have lifted, let alone fired, such a weapon.

<*Let's move,*> Corporal Silva, the fireteam's leader, ordered.

Rika turned and followed the other two scout mechs in her fireteam as they sprinted out of the camp toward the ridge. They kept their run to a sedate 30km/h so as not to kick up dust in the arid hills and alert the enemy to their movement.

It was a shame, too; the double-kneed legs—reminiscent of a horse's hindquarters—were able to propel the SMI-2 mechs over 100km/h, and a full-bore run was one of the few true joys Rika had in life anymore. It was the one time she could pretend she was free.

Ahead of her, Corporal Silva and PFC Kelly loped along a dry streambed east of the ridgeline where they would take up position, their lithe bodies wrapped in layers of dusty, matte-grey armor. Only long familiarity with the way they moved allowed Rika to tell the other two women apart. The things they had become were all but indistinguishable from one another; every trace of individuality cut off or covered up.

Some days it took a lot of effort for Rika to think of herself as a woman, not as a machine. The military would be happy if she was subsumed by what they did to her; to become just a cheap brain inside their hardware, little more than a robot. But robots didn't fight as well as humans—not unless they were powered by AIs, and AIs were expensive and used for much more important tasks. Mech-meat, someone dumb enough to take military service over prison, was cheap.

It was Silva who had saved her, kept her sane. The corporal used to be a waitress—back in 'the world', as they called their former lives. She had been taking acting and dance classes at night, trying to make a life for herself. But the war was taking its toll everywhere. Times got tough, and she palmed a few credit chits, only to find herself standing before a judge, facing a prison sentence or military enlistment.

But somehow Silva's spirit and sense of self were unaffected by what had been done to her—to them. She had forged Rika and Kelly into a team and given them a name: Hammerfall. Now Rika didn't fight for the Genevian Military. She fought for her teammates, her sisters. She would do anything for them.

<*What's the expected enemy strength?*> Rika asked Corporal Silva.

She raised the question on the fireteam's private combat net, a direct and constantly open connection to Silva and Kelly's minds—so long as they were in RF range.

<*Army Intel thinks there are going to be three hundred Niets out there—at least. Medium armor, light troop transports,*> Silva replied. <*Nothing we can't handle if we have to.*>

<*There ain't nothing we can't handle.*> Private Kelly added the team's motto to the conversation.

<*Hammerfall will bring the pain.*> Rika gave the counter call.

The three women all shared a mental smile as they worked their way through the thick brush to the ridge.

The Genevian military frowned on things like names for mech fireteams—hells, they frowned on their mechanized warriors having, let alone using, names at all. But Gunnery Sergeant Myers had more important things to do than to listen in on the three women talk over the Link—or if he did listen in, he didn't care that they used their names from back in the world. Or that they had named their fireteam.

Either way, Rika didn't care. What were they going to do to her team that hadn't been done already?

<What if we just take them all out?> Kelly asked. *<Think Gunny will be pissed?>*

<Don't even think about it,> Corporal Silva replied, and Rika could see her shake the faceless orb that was her helmeted head. *<We have to make sure the squishies get their glory.>*

<Fucking squishies,> Rika added.

She wondered if the army reviled the full-sized mech warriors like they did the scouts. Most mechs were massive, lumbering things, the shells of humans embedded within them. A full-sized mech could tear a ground vehicle in half with its arms, not to mention what one could do with the multiple weapons systems they carried.

The SMI-2 model that Rika and the other two members of team Hammerfall had been turned into was a new experiment by the military. Take smaller humans—namely women—and make a scout mech. A warrior that could carry a significant armament, but operate in environments and terrain that a full-sized mech could not. SMI-2s averaged 2.3 meters in height, and weighed in at no more than 230 kilograms, depending on their loadout. And though more of their human body remained beneath than with a regular mech, their bones and muscles were heavily augmented to give them the strength of a dozen squishies.

<I wonder if they'll have any supplies? Maybe even Nutri-Stations. I bet their paste tastes better than ours,> Kelly said as they neared the top of the ridge.

<Paste doesn't taste,> Rika replied with a mental snort. *<That crap goes right into your stomach. You haven't tasted anything since your last meal before you got caught.>*

Kelly laughed in response. <*Last meal I had was a dick I was sucking in an alley on Kidra, before I got picked up in a sting.*>

Kelly's delivery was crass—as always—but the sentiment was one Rika shared. All the mechs she knew had been picked up for petty crimes. Her own had been stealing food; food she never even got a taste of.

<*Probably why paste doesn't sit well with you, Kelly,*> Silva chuckled in their minds. <*I bet it doesn't go well with all that spunk you're still digesting.*>

<*What a lovely picture,*> Rika said and attempted to shift the conversation. <*I don't know about you, but when I get out, I'm going to eat so much pie and ice cream that I'll get fat as a pig.*>

<*I want coffee,*> Kelly said. <*Fuck, do I want coffee. I'm just going to pour it down my throat for days.*>

<*You're going to need a face for that again,*> Silva said, her voice dropping.

<*They'll give us faces when we get out,*> Kelly insisted. <*I heard it from one of the lieutenants. They're going to put us back together again. Make us real women, not…*> She left the words hanging. None of them wanted to think too much about what they were.

Rika wasn't as optimistic. Their forced enlistment term was five years, but she didn't see a happy ending to the war with the Nietzscheans. It had already been going on for seven years, and her side seemed to be losing ground.

No one spoke of it, but station-by-station, world-by-world, the Niets were pushing them back.

Even if the Genevians did win—in a stalemate, or some miracle victory—they had put too much time and effort into their mechs. They always talked about how the mechs—especially the women in the SMI-2 modules—were just barely adequate, called the humans within 'mech-meat'; but Rika knew better. She had only been in four combat engagements in her six months of service, but each time, it had been the mechs who had saved the day.

Without their firepower and fortitude, the squishies would be doomed.

<*Think the Niets will make us people again if they win?*> Rika asked her teammates.

<*You know Nietzschean philosophy,*> Kelly replied. <*They revile our people for compassion, mercy, all that shit. To them, Genevians have a slave morality—imagine*

what they think of us mechs? To them, we're the slaves of slaves.>

<*For a ten-chit prostitute, you sure know your philosophy,*> Silva said with a laugh.

<*I wasn't always…that.*> Kelly's voice was sullen. <*I had a life before the war came, you know. No matter what, I'm going to get through this war and see my children again—even if I don't get my face back.*>

<*Sorry,*> Silva apologized. <*That came out a bit harsher than I meant it to.*>

<*We all have bad days,*> Kelly said after a pause. <*It's OK.*>

<*Thanks.*>

The women fell silent for a few minutes as they picked their way along the hillside, just a few meters below the ridge, at the military crest. Rika knew what the women all feared, what made them lash out at times. They worried that the best-case scenario was that after the war, the military would remove their compliance chips and military hardware, but that would be all. They'd face a lifetime of slinging cargo in some shit station, saving credits for repairs, power, and NutriPaste.

<*I dream of steak every night,*> Rika finally said, desperate to think of something happy. <*It's juicy, red; mmm… I can almost taste it.*>

<*Mech-meat doesn't dream!*> Silva said in her best mental approximation of Gunnery Sergeant Myer's voice.

<*I dream,*> Kelly said wistfully. <*I dream that they'll add some sort of pleasure attachment to while away the hours when we're on the charging stations.*>

<*Kelly! Seriously!*> Rika exclaimed.

<*We probably don't have enough bits down there anymore for that,*> Silva said morosely. <*Face it, girls: a good time with a man—or a woman—isn't in our future anytime soon.*>

<*Believe it or not, we do still have the parts,*> Rika said. <*I was awake for most of it; I know what they cut, and what they left. And why. Same reason we still have our breasts. My assembler told me that someone up the chain figured that our protective female instincts would be valuable—though the assembler said it was really just to make sure we didn't have crazy hormone imbalances that they'd have to constantly drug us for.*>

Kelly turned the nearly featureless oval that was her head to look back at Rika—an unnecessary gesture since their mods allowed the women to all see in every direction at once.

*<Seriously? You were **awake**? You never told me that!>*

Rika nodded. *<Yeah… I guess I haven't really shared that yet. I wasn't awake for all of it…but I was for the first part, and then the end. We have more face left than you'd think under these.>* She reached up to knock her fist against her head. *<They just want us to **think** we're nothing more than machines.>*

<For the first part…> Silva whispered. *<That's hard-core, Rika…. I had no idea.>*

<Not something I really like to talk about,> Rika replied quietly.

The three women fell silent once more, and Rika did her best to push all thoughts of 'the world' from her mind.

This was one area where she learned that the military knew what they were talking about. As much as she hated to, when it came to combat, it was best to think of herself as a machine. She was capabilities and tactics. She was cold steel and death. Her right arm was her sword, and her thick armor was her shield. She would complete her objectives and return alive.

They reached a small depression in the ridgeline, a saddle where some small scrubby bushes grew, and Silva held up her right hand in a fist.

<OK, girls, let's take a peek and see what it looks like out there.>

They had all been through VR sims of the terrain on the other side of the ridge, they knew its features by heart; but one thing the three women had learned from their prior engagements, is that what the VR showed was someone else's impression of what was important.

Little details always seemed to be off, and those little details made all the difference on the ground.

It could be something as small as a bush, or the degree to which a tree's limbs bent in a wind. How much dust was on the ground for the enemy to kick up…anything could make the difference between coming back, and being just another rotting corpse on the battlefield.

Silva took a position on the left side of the saddle, Kelly on the right, and Rika crouched low behind a boulder in the middle.

Below them, stretching off into the west, was a broad plain. It was shrouded in early morning shadow; the ridge still obscuring the growing light of Parson, the system's star, which rose behind them in the east. Wind rushed across the dry plain, creating small dunes and eddies of dry earth as it whipped around stray rock outcroppings and a few stunted trees.

A road—little more than a single lane of packed dirt—twisted its way toward the ridgeline from the west before running alongside it for a few kilometers.

It was a wide-open killbox.

She wondered why the Nietzscheans would travel on the west side of the ridge, and not in the hill country to the east. Military strategy was not something they taught much of during her indoctrination, but Rika supposed that if you were worried about an ambush—and everyone was always worried about ambushes—having just one ridgeline looming over you was better than two.

Even so, two kilometers to the north, the road the enemy was traveling on crossed into the hills, and that was where the bulk of Alpha Company would hit them.

<I see them,> Kelly said, and passed the coordinates over the Link to the other members of team Hammerfall.

Rika cycled her vision to a higher level of magnification and saw a thin cloud of dust rising off the plain.

<Rate of travel, just twenty kph,> Rika estimated. *<Slow.>*

<Yeah,> Silva agreed. *<Passing this on to the gunny. Kelly, you stay here. Rika, I want you to find a good spot a few hundred meters to the south; I'll take a position to the north. We don't fire till the company hits them. Then we'll pick 'em off from the rear.>*

<And save everyone's asses again,> Kelly muttered.

<Think we'll get any help from fleet?> Rika asked.

<Doubt it,> Silva replied. *<I overheard one of the LT's talking back at camp. They're pretty evenly matched up there; neither side is getting close to the planet, other than sneaking ground forced down when they can. What we have down here is all we got.>*

<So, just like normal,> Kelly chuckled.

<Yeah. Now get moving, Rika. They'll be here soon.>

Rika nodded her assent and slipped out of the saddle, back to the eastern side of the ridge.

She was glad the fleets were holding back. Naera was the last terrestrial world that the Genevians held in the Parson System. If they lost it, it was probable that the entire system would fall to the Nietzscheans in a matter of weeks. The Niets won in space more often than not, which meant that if ships showed up to rain starfire, it would probably come down on the Genevians.

The Niets were fierce warriors on the ground, as well. When it came down to squishie versus squishie, they tended to win. However, now that the Genevians were employing mech-meat, the tables had turned, and the Genevians were seeing more victories than losses, when the fighting happened dirt-side.

Still, all too often, the ground forces would see their victory rendered meaningless by the fleets falling back and abandoning whatever territory they had secured. Or an orbital strike from the Niets would render the victory moot—like what had happened to Bravo Company.

Ahead, Rika spotted a series of granite outcroppings, something that could offer real cover if the enemy spotted her and fired back. Who was she kidding? *When* the enemy spotted her and fired back.

She lay prone and extended her right arm over the top of a low slab of green granite. She didn't need her head to be above the rock; she could 'see' through the rifle's optical sights without exposing anything more than the weapon's barrel.

Rika took another look at the enemy's rate of travel, and estimated that they would pass in front of her in five minutes; and then reach Bravo Company's ambush site two minutes later.

She signaled her passel of remote drones to deploy around her, directing them a hundred meters up and down the ridge, extra eyes to make sure no one would sneak up on her. They also facilitated lower EM level comms with the rest of Hammerfall. She didn't need to send a message the half kilometer to Silva—only just as far as the closest drone, relaying comms through short hops using tightbeam signals.

Over the next minute, as the enemy grew closer, she could make out more of the enemy formation through the cloud of dust they kicked up. Two lumbering figures were visible through the haze, and Rika realized they were mechs—one at the fore, the other at the rear of the column.

Everything she knew said the Nietzscheans despised mechs; their true warrior code would never allow any of them to submit such an indignity. Perhaps their continual losses on the ground to the Genevian mechs had made them reconsider.

*No…*she thought as a gust of wind blew the dust away from the mech at the front of the enemy column. That was no Nietzschean mech; it was Genevian. The enemy, it seemed, had no compunctions about using captured Genevians. Though Rika supposed that it fit with their master-slave morality. If the Genevians were willing to create a slave class, the Nietzscheans would be more than happy to make use of it.

Rika looked at the mech and compared its buildout to what she knew of other models the Genevian military produced. It most closely resembled a K1R, though there were a few alterations to suit Nietzschean weaponry.

<*See that?*> Rika sent to her team through her relay drones. She included a visual of the mech with her message.

<*Oh, shit!*> Silva replied. <*I couldn't make that out from my position.*>

<*K1R, right?*> Kelly asked.

<*Looks like it,*> Rika answered. <*But that heavy slug thrower on its right arm looks like it's a higher caliber, and they've removed the sensor dome from the top…must be those nodules on its chest and shoulders.*>

<*That's gonna put a crimp in the CO's plans,*> Silva commented. <*I'll relay this back to Gunny.*>

<*Do we even have the firepower to take out a K1R?*> Kelly asked. <*And how did the Niets capture one? Normally the only way to stop those things is to rip 'em to shreds.*>

<*Two,*> Rika replied.

<*Two?*>

<*Yeah, there's another at the rear of the column. I bet we're going to get to tangle with that one,*> Rika said with a sigh.

<*Well, shit,*> Kelly swore. <*I shoulda stayed in bed.*>

<You don't have a bed,> Rika chuckled. *<You have a rack, and it's a mess.>*

<That's not my fault! One of the techs spilled lubricant all over, and dirt stuck to it!>

<Girls! Focus,> Silva sent back. *<Gunny has new orders for us. As soon as they hit the front of the column, we're to unload on the K1R in the rear. Eliminate with extreme prejudice.>*

<Sure, send in the meat,> Kelly grunted. *<How are they going to take out the one in the front?>*

<Company has a dozen SAWs,> Silva replied. *<They should be able to do the trick.>*

Poor bastards, Rika thought with a shake of her head as she watched the K1R mech lumbering at the head of the column. *We're just hardware in this fight. Whoever picks us up off the ground gets to pull our trigger.*

<Stay frosty, girls,> Silva said. *<When it closes with one of us, and it* **will** *close with someone, we come to her aid. Got it?>*

<Got it. Ain't nothing we can't handle,> Rika replied.

<Damn straight, Hammerfall brings the pain.> Kelly added.

None of the women spoke further as the column approached and began to pass below the ridge, just three hundred meters down the slope, and another half-klick out on the plain. Roughly seven hundred meters as the projectile—or beam—flew.

<*Silva,*> Rika messaged the corporal as the rear of the column passed her position. <*With the K1Rs down there, do we have authorization to use proton beams?*>

<*Negative,*> Silva replied. <*Apparently, they still want shit to be able to live on this planet when we're done.*>

<*Really?*> Kelly asked. <*Shit barely grows here as it is.*>

<*I think that's the point,*> Silva replied. <*Electron beams only—and your kinetics and projectiles, of course.*>

<*Roger,*> Rika sent back.

None of those weapons would take down a K1R before it knew where you were. Electron beams would be the best, but those drew a straight blue-white bolt of lightning between the weapon and the target—a big arrow telling the enemy where to shoot.

They also heavily sapped the tiny bottle of antimatter each of the three women carried within their torsos. When that antimatter bottle ran dry, they would be down to superconductor batteries; and those wouldn't power their armor or weapons for long.

If the fleet was nearby, they could beam energy down to their mechs, but they all knew that wasn't going to happen. They'd have to take down the K1R's the old-fashioned way.

A swath of enemy drones flew up over the ridge, scanning the area for enemies, and Rika clenched her jaw—or at least the neural feedback from her augmentations told her she was clenching her jaw—praying that her active camouflage would hide her from the prying eyes above.

The enemy didn't halt their march, and she knew she was safe for the moment. Down on the plain, the head of the column had almost reached the pass into the hills. Rika forced her breathing to slow as she waited for the opening salvos—which would be the sound of Alpha Company's SAWs opening up on the K1R in the lead.

Rika took a moment to wonder, now that they had their own mechs, if the Nietzscheans did have Nutri-Stations. Maybe their paste *was* better. Though Rika and Silva needled Kelly about it, she was right; half the time they all felt ill after 'eating'.

Her momentary distraction ended as the thundering *CRACK-CRACK-CRACK* of the SAWs echoed through the hills, and Rika wasted no time opening fire on the K1R in the rear with her GNR-41B sniper rifle.

She used its kinetic projectile firing mode and mentally squeezed the trigger. The weapon launched a quintet of 22cm projectiles that burst from its muzzle with little more than a soft snap. The rounds flew across the thousand meters to her target in three tenths of a second, striking the target with a combined 1.5 billion joules of kinetic energy.

She had aimed for the joint where the K1R's right leg attached to its torso, but the shot missed, striking the mech's 'thigh' instead. The beast of a machine barely flinched as the rounds struck it, and it turned toward her just as it was hit by Kelly and Silva's rounds.

Kelly's shots hit the mech in the upper 'chest', smashing one of its sensor nodules, while Silva's traced a line down its torso; one lucky round hitting the K1R's hip joint, though it did not appear to sustain any noticeable damage.

The K1R turned and aimed both its weapons at the hillside. It took a moment to triangulate the origin of the incoming projectiles, before firing three shots from its 50mm canon. Depleted uranium rods burst from sabots and screamed through the dawn air and slammed into the top of the ridge.

The women of team Hammerfall had not stuck around to see if their cover could withstand those rounds, and were well below the top of the ridgeline, on the move to new positions when they hit.

Rika released another passel of drones, these ones larger and equipped with lasers. They fired at the enemy surveillance drones, and while she took up a new position; automated aerial combat took place above her.

She pulled the feed from her first batch of drones, and saw that the enemy column had stopped. The K1R was spraying the hillside with covering fire as

Nietzschean troops in fully powered battle armor leapt out of the transports.

<*Shit!*> Kelly called over the Link. <*That's not medium armor! This ambush is an ambush!*>

Rika sent affirmation back to her teammate. Soldiers in full armor didn't need transports. They could run as fast as the trucks could drive—faster if they had jump-jets. One on one, the Nietzscheans still weren't a match for the SMI-2s of team Hammerfall; but they were still a force to be reckoned with—especially when there were three hundred of them.

<*I'll keep those Niets pinned down,*> Silva called out. <*You two take down that K1R before it tears up the whole hillside.*>

<*Going to beams,*> Rika announced, and switched her GNR-41B to the electron beam mode, causing the second barrel to rotate into firing position.

She aligned it with the K1R's torso, right where two of the armor plates overlapped, hoping to slip the beam in for a kill shot.

She fired, and for a fraction of a second, a laser lanced between her rifle and the target, superheating the air and opening a path for the electrons; then the beam fired. A blue-white bolt of lightning described a straight line between Rika and the K1R mech. A nimbus haze of Cerenkov radiation glowed around the beam—a result, she was told—of the electrons scattering as they collided with the atoms in the air.

The K1R was at the edge of the beam's effective range, but a stream of electrons travelling close to the speed of light still packed a huge punch, even if it spread out over few centimeters before it hit the target.

Her shot was true, and the beam hit where the armor overlapped in a blinding flash of light, as bolts of lightning arched through the air around the K1R. A second later, Kelly fired her electron beam as well, hitting the same spot on the K1R, and their combined strikes burned a hole through the first layer of ablative plating.

As an added bonus, the radiation showering off the mech caused the Nietzscheans nearby to back away to a safe distance. They bunched up, and down the ridgeline, Silva fired her own electron beam into their midst, scattering them once more.

In response to their attack, the K1R fired a single missile from the launcher on its back. It flew high overhead, almost disappearing from view, before it turned and streaked down from the heavens toward the positions Rika and Kelly had vacated after firing their electron beams.

If the K1R meant to take them out with one missile, it was going to be a big one, and Rika sprinted away at top speed, hoping that Kelly had the sense to do the same. She was half a kilometer from her previous location when a blinding light appeared a dozen meters off the ground.

She ducked behind a large rock and gripped the ground with the three claws on each of her feet as the nuclear shockwave, and the hot, radioactive wind which followed, washed over her.

Fuck! Tacnukes! So much for a livable world. The Nietzscheans were pulling out all the stops. She thanked the stars that she was leeward from the wind, and allowed a minute for the stiff breeze to blow away at least some of the fallout before she peered around the rock.

<*Kelly! Silva!*> Rika called out, doubtful that they could pick her up through the irradiated

atmosphere. She pinged her drones and only two responded. She directed them toward her teammates' positions, hoping to pick up a signal as she released her final passel to aid in the search.

She looked at the rock she had taken cover behind, and took a second to appreciate that nearly half of it had melted away. The ground between her and the ridge was a smoking ruin, shrouded by the mushroom cloud that rose overhead.

A note on her HUD provided an estimate as to the weapon's probable yield: 100 kilotons. More than enough to melt through an SMI2's armor and fry the meat inside.

<Rika! Are you alive?> came a call from Kelly, relayed through one of Rika's drones.

<Yes, amazingly! Are you hurt? That was a fucking nuke!>

<No shit! My cover wasn't big enough, blast melted the end off my GNR!> Kelly added a string of curses directed at the K1R and his heritage before asking, *<Have you reached Silva?>*

<No,> Rika replied as she cast a worried eye toward the ridge. In a minute, the K1R was going to come over the top; she prayed it didn't have another

tacnuke in his back pocket, because that wasn't the sort of ordinance she wanted to dodge again.

As if on cue, the mech topped the rise; its four-meter height a dark shadow in the dim morning sun, further obscured by the dust and ash in the air from the nuclear blast.

<*Aw, fuck!*> Rika swore as the K1R spotted her and unleashed several rounds from its 50mm cannon.

She dashed up the smoldering valley's far slope at top speed, aiming to put another rise between her and the enemy.

<*I'll draw it,*> Kelly called out. <*You get up there and give me cover to get up after you.*>

<*Kelly, no! Your nine-seven can't even scratch a K1R at that range,*> Rika responded, referring to the AR97 secondary weapon the SMI-2s carried. It was a standard Genevian multi-purpose weapon, the sort that the heavy weapons squishies might use, but not much more than a spitgun when it came to taking on a K1R at anything other than point-blank range.

The bark of Kelly's AR97 confirmed that Rika's teammate wasn't going to heed her advice. She decided not to waste Kelly's bravery, and made the top of the next rise before dashing down the far side then north fifty meters, and back up, where she fired her electron beam at the mech once more.

Her probes had kept it in sight, and she only needed a second to lock onto the monster and strike it once more at the same place as before.

The mech took the hit, and, after the shower of sparks and lightning, its left arm began to jerk erratically. Rika gave thanks that no more 50mm rounds would come their way. While her beam rifle recharged, she pulled the AR97 off its latch on her back and fired from the hip with its 15mm rounds. She spent the clip in twenty seconds while the K1R on the far rise fought with its spasming limb.

Rika was glad to see that Kelly made proper use of the distraction, and raced up the rise, discarding the twisted barrel of her GNR-41B's sniper rifle in her wake.

Once her teammate was over the ridge, Rika dashed down the far side of the slope and met up with her.

<Just the barrel was exposed? Are you sure?> she asked, while looking Kelly over.

<*Yes, mom, I'm sure,*> Kelly replied while she pulled the rest of the GNR-41B's assembly off. Once it was clear, Kelly slapped her AR97 into the gun mount, and drew her DR88 handgun free from its thigh-holster.

<*Strat?*> Rika asked.

<*Cat and mouse. We keep popping up and taking pot shots. I'll try to keep its focus on me, so that you can kick it in the face with your beam.*>

<*Just don't be reckless, Kelly. We girls have to stick together.*>

Kelly cocked her grey oval head. <*Reckless, Rika? I wouldn't dream of it.*>

Rika gave a mental snort as Kelly turned and raced a hundred meters to the north before cresting the rise and opening fire with her AR97. Rika didn't waste any time, moving to the south and lining up to fire as the K1R fired a salvo from its heavy repeater at Kelly.

Her teammate dodged the first few shots, but then one ricocheted off her arm and spun her around.

<*Thought you were going to be careful?*> Rika asked as her electron beam lanced out, striking the

corresponding location on the other side of the mech's torso.

<That ***was*** *careful! That thing is mad and fast.>* Kelly replied as she ran to a new position. *<No damage, though; was a glancing impact.>*

<I saw one of your ablative plates fly off!> Rika called back as she moved into new cover as well. *<Don't tell me 'no damage'.>*

<It's ablative, it ablated,> Kelly replied with a chuckle.

Rika watched the K1R through the eyes of her drones as it descended into the valley and began to climb the slope toward Kelly's position. She braced herself to make another shot, when the enemy mech leapt into the air, powerful chem boosters pushing it up over the rise to land just five meters away from Kelly.

<Fawk!> Kelly screamed as she unloaded her AR97 rifle's kinetic rounds into the K1R while backpedaling and firing her DR88 handgun at full auto.

The enemy hunched forward, ignoring the weapons fire, intent on getting its massive hands around the SMI-2 mech in front of it.

Rika didn't give a moment's thought as she rushed toward the K1R, her double-kneed legs pushing her up over a hundred kilometers per hour. When she was twenty meters away, she leapt, barely passing over a stream of projectile fire the enemy casually sprayed in her direction as it grabbed Kelly by her right arm.

She landed on the K1R, the claws on her feet clamping onto its shoulders. Rika switched modes on her AR97, and fired a stream of rail-accelerated pellets into the joints where the K1R's arms met its body. Half the pellets ricocheted off—a few striking her own armor—but she kept firing. Four seconds later, the enemy mech's left arm—the one dangling Kelly's body in the air—fell limp.

Kelly crashed to the ground, and the K1R began to flail wildly, attempting to shake Rika free as she continued to fire into its body. She spent a second clip, and then crouched low and leapt straight up, firing her electron beam at point-blank range.

With few atmospheric nuclei between her weapon and the target, the bolt of electrons tore through the front of the K1R, splitting its torso wide open.

Rika landed on the ground in front of the K1R as the massive metal monster fell backwards.

She turned to Kelly, who was struggling to her feet; her right arm a mangled mess of twisted carbon and steel and soaked in blood.

<I'm good,> Kelly said, though her mental tone told Rika a different story.

Rika made a move toward her teammate, but Kelly waved her off.

<Seriously, check the K1R. Put that thing down for good.>

Rika nodded and turned back to the mech, half-curious, half-scared to see what was inside. She knew that the K1R models were skinners…meaning that they still wore human skin inside their cocoon. If they weren't pulled out and cleaned with some frequency—something that rarely happened in the field—they would be a stinking mess.

She approached the fallen enemy and saw that her beam had cut clear through to the cocoon inside. Rika slipped her AR97 back onto its latch before gripping one side of the gash with her right foot, while pulling on the other side with her left hand.

With a deafening shriek, the split widened enough that she could see the person—a man, from the looks of it—inside. He certainly lived up to the 'mech-meat' moniker. He was nothing more than a limbless torso, covered in bright red, welt-covered skin. Pus oozed from sores, mostly around the bio ports on his body, where cables and tubes just punctured his flesh wherever it was convenient.

<*Shiiiiit,*> Kelly whispered from behind her.

Rika didn't know what to say to the ruin of a man. Only one thing came to mind, and she activated her external speakers.

"I'm sorry." The artificial voice the Genevian military had granted her grated out the toneless words.

The man had a pair of tubes going down his throat, but it seemed he possessed the ability to speak audibly as a mechanical voice rasped, "What are you waiting for? Do it."

"How did they turn you?" Kelly asked. "How can you kill your people?"

"What does it matter," the ruined man said from within the K1R's cocoon. "We're all just meat. All we do is kill. You, them; it doesn't matter. It's what we are now. Killers."

Rika heard his words—angry, resolute—but his eyes said something else. They held a pain she knew all too well.

The man was right about one thing: they were killers.

She took a step back and switched her GNR-41B to its projectile mode before leveling the barrel at his head. Rika whispered through her suit's speakers, "I release you."

The weapon gave its nearly inaudible snap, and the man's head exploded.

Rika turned away, but her three-sixty vision didn't let her stop seeing it. She focused on Kelly, wishing she had never seen the thing inside the armor behind her.

It was a fate none of them deserved, but which they would all earn in the end.

OVERWHELMED

STELLAR DATE: 12.01.8941 (Adjusted Years)
LOCATION: Western plains of Naera
REGION: Parson System, Genevian Federation

Weapons fire came from the ridge to the west, and the *SNAP-PING* of projectiles hitting the ground around them brought the two women back to their senses.

They dove behind the K1R's fallen mass and surveyed their surroundings. At least nine of the Nietzscheans in powered armor stood atop the rise, raining fire down on them. Rika would bet her bottom dollar—if she got paid for this shit—that there enemies out there as well, moving in to flank them.

Rika slid the barrel of her sniper rifle over the fallen mech's body and fired a pair of depleted uranium rods at one of the Nietzscheans, and then a second pair of rods at another. The rods struck true, and both of the targets were picked up and flung off the ridge by the force of the impacts.

<Nice shooting, Rika,> Kelly said, appreciation filling her mental tone. *<And thanks for saving my ass from the K1R. Another few seconds, and he was going to tear me in half.>*

<You can thank me in the afterlife,> Rika replied as she ducked down behind the K1R's steel corpse. *<We're pinned down here and there're two companies of those Niets coming for us.>*

<Nah,> Silva's welcome voice filled their minds. *<Just a couple of platoons. The rest are fighting the squishies.>*

<Sil!> Rika and Kelly called out in unison.

<Live and in living color. Stay low, I'm going to throw those assholes on the ridge a party.>

Rika and Kelly fell prone. A party was team Hammerfall's name for the special grenades only the fireteam leads got. Parties detonated in the air and small, guided packets flew out and attached to enemy targets—most often the head if they could manage.

Once attached, the packets ignited a thermite charge and burned clear through whatever they were stuck to. The mad flailing dance anyone unfortunate enough to be near a party when it went off was what caused the women to give it the name.

A second later, they heard the resounding crack as the party exploded—the screaming wasn't far behind. Rika watched through her drones as seven of the Niets began tearing off their armor. They gave it a three-count before she and Kelly fired on the other five enemies, who also were frantically checking themselves over.

Ten seconds later, all twelve Nietzschean soldiers were down. Either from the party, the three women's weapons fire, or the extreme levels of radiation that waited for them outside of their armor from both the nuke and Rika's liberal use of her electron beam.

<*Let's move, girls,*> Silva called out as she slipped over the ridgeline toward Kelly and Rika. <*Gunny wants us to hook back up with the company and save their asses.*>

<*Did they take out their K1R?*> Kelly asked as the three women began to sprint north through the valley.

<*Yeah, but the sitrep I got from him said they lost two dozen doing it—and it didn't even fire its tacnuke,*>

Silva replied, her mental tone a mixture of sorrow for the loss of their comrades, and pride for her team's efficiency.

Rika didn't share the sentimental feelings Silva displayed; maybe because Silva had been a real member of society with a future back in the world. Rika had never even had a home or a family. If it weren't for the brutal mutilation of her body and the compliance chip in her head, the military would be a step up from her prior life.

Which wasn't saying much at all.

Sometimes she wondered if she should stop fighting so hard and pray that the Nietzscheans would win. Although, after seeing the meat in that K1R, she was certain that the Niets wouldn't be any better than the Genevians. Maybe they could both lose equally and she could figure out a way to get free.

Rika shook her head. Every option was shit. All that mattered was just surviving today so that she could make it to tomorrow. At some point, it had to get better.

Silva led them along a route that paralleled the one they took on the way out—just one valley to the east. Behind them, Rika's probes picked up movement; probably the flanking troops that were going to hit them before Silva threw the party.

The enemy was almost a kilometer to their rear, but that was well within weapons range. She signaled for the others to take cover as she sent a probe high over the valley to get a clear view.

Sure enough, an enemy platoon with good camo gear was picking its way toward them. These soldiers had different armor than the ones in the convoy—scout gear, not heavy, fully-powered stuff. Though their armor was weaker, scout troops were usually better soldiers. Unlike the ones who stood on ridgelines to fire—they were just FNG cannon fodder.

<There's a ravine ahead that leads to the next valley to the east,> Kelly offered. *<We could slip through that and mine the shit out of it. When they follow…>* she splayed her arms apart; a gesture that lost something in translation with her AR97 attached to her gun mount, and her other arm a mangled ruin.

<You realize you're bleeding all over your tech,> Silva said, her voice taking on a motherly tone.

<Its almost stopped,> Kelly said *<The nano is just flushing some of the rads out of my bloodstream. Once it finishes, it'll biofoam it all up.>*

<Keep an eye on your blood pressure,> Silva warned. *<I don't want you fainting on us. Rika will have to carry your sorry ass, and she hates doing that.>*

Rika said with a mental smile. *<It's like a habit at this point.>*

<Was just that one fucking time,> Kelly swore and shook her head.

Silva rose from her cover and crept toward the ravine.

<Keep that arm low, Kelly; its camo is shot. Let's go 'mine the shit out of' the ravine, as you so gracefully put it, and then pick off any assholes that make it through.>

In short order, the three women had planted their full supply of mines in the ravine and along the eastern slopes on either side of it—just in case any of the enemy scouts went around the gorge. Which they should, if they were smart.

All told, twenty-eight hidden explosives waited for the enemy. After taking up positions behind three separate piles of rock on the east side of the valley, they settled in to wait.

Less than five minutes later, Rika caught sight of an enemy drone as it crested the hill. She was surprised it was so easy to spot; but then she realized that the enemy probably expected ambush, and the drones were scanning the ground.

She pulled a feed from team Hammerfall's drones, which were almost a kilometer overhead at this point—except for a few comm relay units, which sat on the ground between their positions. From there, she could see that the enemy drones, by some miracle, had missed their mines. She prayed that the enemy troops wouldn't follow the paths of their drones too closely.

The mines gave off no EM signatures, and unless the enemy was running ground sonar with every step—something that would give the soldiers away like a beacon in the night—they wouldn't be able to spot the mines.

Through her overhead view, Rika saw a few of the enemy troops begin to enter the ravine, while the rest scaled the hillsides.

She didn't envy the poor assholes that had to go through the narrow gash between the hills, but she knew it was necessary. Their team had to clear it. If they didn't, they'd never know if their enemy was hiding within, waiting either to strike them from the rear, or to slip off to the west and escape.

Then, just when she began to wonder if the Nietzscheans in the ravine had turned around to back out, one of the mines detonated. A cry rose up, and then several more mines exploded—likely the ones to the rear that were placed to block a rapid retreat.

As the women watched, several of the Nietzschean scouts came over the ridge, staying low and using cover well enough that they would be almost impossible to hit. Rika wondered if maybe their drones had managed to detect the hidden explosives; she was getting ready to fire her GNR, when another mine went off. This time there was no scream as one of the Niet's bodies flew into the air, and the scouts on the hillside all froze in place.

<That's right, assholes,> Kelly said with a wicked grin visible over the Link, *<we thought of that, too.>*

<Rika, fire on targets of opportunity,> Silva announced, and picked off one of the scouts that was slowly moving to a new position on the hillside.

Rika sent several rounds toward the enemy, killing two before she ran out of clear targets. She was considering moving to a new position, when Gunnery Sergeant Myer's voice broke into their minds.

<*Where the fuck are you bitches? We're getting torn up, here!*>

<*We're coming, sir,*> Silva replied. <*Just have a 'toon of bad guys on our tail that we didn't think you wanted joining in.*>

<*Fine, get rid of them ASAP. I expect to see your skinny asses here in five minutes. Or else.*>

Rika knew what the 'or else' meant. Even from this range, it was no problem for the gunnery sergeant to trigger Discipline, something that could get them killed if they were in combat. The gunny also wasn't afraid to use the chip's max setting—something that hurt worse than getting shot. Rika knew; she had experienced both.

<*Kelly, you're on bait duty. Run up the hill behind us and see if any of them get excited enough to follow you,*> Silva ordered.

<*Fiiine,*> Kelly replied. <*But next time, Rika gets to hide behind the small rock when the nuke goes off.*>

She stayed low, moving up the slope from cover to cover. Rika appreciated her caution. There was a difference between playing bait, and getting your ass shot off.

Just as they'd hoped, a few of the enemy scouts picked up the movement and leaned out of cover to fire. Five shots lanced out from Rika and Silva's GNR-41B's, and there were five fewer enemies.

<What do you estimate?> Rika asked. *<Ten total?>*

<Could be more, from the blasts in the ravine,> Silva replied. *<We haven't seen any movement in there since this started.>*

<A third of their platoon dead in five minutes seems suitably demoralizing,> Kelly said. *<I think we can move on—we have the drones watching.>*

<Cover me,> Silva said to Rika as she moved up the hillside.

Rika nodded and moved to a new position before sliding her GNR-41B's barrel over a rock and firing a trio of depleted uranium rounds at locations where her drones had spotted movement. By the time the rods slammed into the rocks on the far side of the valley, Silva was halfway up the slope. A few seconds later and the corporal was over the ridge with Kelly.

<*OK,*> Rika replied, and slipped out from her cover, carefully moving up the slope as Silva fired a quartet of rounds from above her. She was almost over the ridge when a *SNAP* sounded nearby, and she felt a searing pain in her right leg.

She looked down and saw a chunk of her left thigh missing. *Great, I just have to get hit in the tiny part of my leg that's not steel.* She dropped down and clawed her way over the hilltop before rolling onto her back, wishing she could do something like wince or grind her teeth, as biofoam spilled out of her armor and sealed the wound.

Silva rushed to her side and grabbed a field kit from her pack.

<*This is going to hurt a bit,*> the corporal said.

<*Just do it already,*> Rika hissed in response.

Silva pulled a support rod from the field kit and pushed it into the biofoam. Once it picked up its location and read her biostats, the support rod expanded in her wound with explosive force. One end anchored into an internal mount at the top of her artificial knee joint, and the other sank into her hip.

Rika clenched and unclenched her left hand while Kelly grabbed the barrel of her GNR-41B to keep it from flailing and hitting Silva.

<*Faaaaaaawk! I thought this thing was supposed to dampen the nerves before it did that!*> Rika swore.

<*From what I can see on your readout, it did,*> Silva replied. <*I had to do this once before on my arm. Your hip is going to be stiff, and move weird. The rod has a ball-joint in it, so you can still bend your leg, but I bet your range of motion is going to be limited.*>

Rika nodded as the biofoam hardened around her leg. Once it set, she struggled to rise. Standing didn't hurt as much as she thought it would, but she wasn't anticipating the two-kilometer hike to where their company was duking it out with the Nietzscheans.

Not to mention going head-to-head with another couple hundred of those bastards.

<*Today, soldier,*> Silva barked. <*Gunny's not going to wait forever.*>

The thought got Rika moving, and she followed Silva and Kelly down the slope as quickly as she could.

Above, her drones kept an eye on the scouts on the other side of the hill—who had not yet moved beyond the minefield. Rika was glad to see that they wouldn't be hit from two sides before tapping into Silva's drones, which had ranged to the edge of the company's beleaguered position.

Upon seeing Alpha Company's position, Rika wished that she could let out a frustrated sigh, or scream, or something.... The squishies were supposed to be the professionals. She and the other members of team Hammerfall had only been out of indoctrination for less than a year, and they got into way fewer binds than the regular soldiers in the Genevian military.

<*Wow, look at those tools,*> Kelly commented, apparently on the same train of thought.

<*I guess it takes a criminal to know how to fight dirty,*> Rika said with a rueful chuckle.

Alpha Company was pinned down at the end of a narrow valley with high, steep slopes—how they got themselves in that position, Rika didn't even want to know. They bore heavy casualties, but over a hundred soldiers were still able to pull a trigger.

<Gunny wants us to circle behind the enemy so we can catch 'em in a crossfire,> Silva said.

<What, he didn't go all-comms again to call us bitches? I'm crushed,> Kelly replied.

Rika chuckled. *<You're just going to have to manage without the gunny's abuse.>*

Fireteam Hammerfall slipped around behind the Nietzschean troops, who were taking their time wearing down the Genevians. Rika didn't blame them. Nothing worse than a cornered enemy. Best to keep one's distance in a situation like this.

Rika settled in behind a wide granite slab a half-kilometer behind the Nietzscheans, and twisted her wounded leg under her so that her functional camo could keep her concealed. Silva was positioned up a hill to her right, and Kelly, whose AR97 lacked the ability to fire accurately over a half-klick, was a few hundred meters closer to the enemy, below their position.

Rika watched the countdown Silva had placed in her HUD, ready to bring fire down on the enemy.

When it reached zero, she waited for Kelly to lob in a couple of parties that Silva had passed out; when the enemy began the traditional dance, Rika fired five of her uranium rods—noting that she only had ten left—before switching to the electron beam, and burning a hole through three enemy soldiers who had lined up nicely for her.

Silva followed a similar strike pattern, and while the two snipers moved to new positions, Kelly fired at close range targets with her AR97 before ducking back behind cover and lobbing another party into the mix.

<*That should give them something to think about,*> Kelly laughed over the Link, while Rika watched the enemy rush to find cover that protected them from the new threat.

On the far side of the Nietzscheans, the soldiers of Alpha Company surged from behind their cover, launching a counter attack on the enemy, taking advantage of their temporary disarray. After less than a minute in the crossfire, the Nietzscheans broke and ran; the Genevians and the three members of team Hammerfall picking off another dozen as they fled.

<Well, that seemed too easy,> Kelly said. *<I mean…they're just squishies, but usually they put up more of a fight before they cut and run.>*

Then one of Rika's drones caught a flash of motion high in the sky and she screamed at Kelly, *<Run!>*

CHANGE OF FATE

STELLAR DATE: 12.01.8941 (Adjusted Years)
LOCATION: Western plains of Naera
REGION: Parson System, Genevian Federation

The nuke detonated directly over Alpha Company, burning the squishies to ash in seconds. Rika crouched behind her cover, praying that Kelly, who was much closer to the explosion, had weathered this second attack.

Seconds ticked by as she waited for team Hammerfall's combat net to come back to life. When it did, Kelly's mental voice was a welcome sound.

<*What's with the nukes?*> Kelly called out. <*The way the Niets fight, there won't be anything left to fight over.*>

Rika peered out from behind her cover, once again thanking the strange blue-green granite on Naera for being so damn hard. The Geiger counter on her HUD was spiking, and she knew that if they didn't wash the radioactive dust off their armor soon, it was going to irradiate their entire bodies.

Down the slope, Kelly was extricating herself from a narrow crevasse, and gave Rika a short wave. *<Seriously, next time I get the good cover.>*

Rika looked past Kelly, down to the narrow end of the valley where Alpha Company had been rushing out after the Nietzscheans. Charred corpses were all that she could see. No one would have survived a blast at that range.

<We gotta move,> Silva ordered. *<Those Niets will wonder if they cooked us, too, and they'll be back here before long to find out. I prefer not to get crispy, so hop to it!>*

<You have such a way with words,> Rika commented.

<That I do, private. Kelly, anything else melted off this time?>

<Funny, Silva,> Kelly said as she trotted up the slope to where Silva waited. *<I thought I might have to tear my right boob off to get out of that little crack in the ground, but it looks like I'm all here.>*

<Good,> Silva nodded as Rika approached. *<You look all in one piece too, Rika. What's your ammo situation look like?>*

<Ten sabot rounds for the GNR, plus two full magazines of projectiles. My antimatter bottle is down to sixty percent, and I've only got ten more mags for my AR97.>

<I'm down to four mags for my AR,> Kelly added. *<But my weapons mount has two-dozen sabots and four mags of projectiles for the GNR.>*

<I'm close to Rika's counts,> Silva said. *<Kelly lay out your extras, and we'll give you a mag each for the AR.>*

The women quickly swapped their ammunition around, and Silva handed out a pair of parties, just in case things got dicey.

<Looks like they're getting curious,> Rika said as her drones updated her feed to show a platoon of fully-armored Nietzscheans moving in from the west.

Rika eyed the Nietzschean weapons lying near the corpses of their kills and wished they could grab some. There just wasn't time to disable the safety locks—and if they didn't, the weapons could detonate when the women picked them up.

<OK, let's move out. We'll head east toward the battalion HQ. I'll try to make a hookup to their net when

we get out from under this radioactive cloud,> Silva announced, and took off at an easy lope.

Rika followed, wincing as the support rod in her leg pulled at her shredded flesh and made her gait ungainly. For the first time, she wished that the Genevian military had taken just a bit more of her body. She remembered wondering, after she came out of the assembly facility, why so much of her remained organic. Some models of mechs were little more than brains in jars; nothing more than cheap AI replacements that the government scooped up off the streets.

The answer had come from one of the drill instructors during her all-to-short time in boot. He explained that human twitch reflexes were honed over decades of use. Whole sections of the brain were dedicated to pulling on the right muscles to get the right movement. Replacing knees and elbows to strengthen those joints was relatively simple, but hips were a lot trickier. It was easier to re-enforce the bones and replace the hip socket with a mechanical joint than to take out all the muscles and nerves.

Plus, it was cheaper and faster.

Rika pushed the memories from her mind, pushed everything from her mind, as she followed Silva and Kelly over the hills and valleys. After fifteen minutes of running, which put over twenty kilometers between them and the site of the tacnuke's explosion—and the remains of Alpha Company—they came down a steep slope into a ravine with a fast-flowing river at its bottom.

Silva called a halt and Rika leaned on a rock, taking the pressure off her right leg.

<*We've probably left a trail a moron could follow,*> Silva said. <*I'm going to scale the far slope and then continue east another klick. Terrain is rockier there, so I can double back and hide my tracks.*>

<*Downstream or upstream?*> Rika asked.

<*Downstream,*> Silva replied. <*I'll meet up with you two klicks to the south.*>

Rika and Kelly nodded before glancing at one another—something that was pointless with their featureless helmets, but they still seemed to do it anyway. Rika knew what Kelly was thinking. They had five hundred kilometers to cross before they got to the battalion HQ, and Silva hadn't said whether or not she had managed to raise them on the comms.

It wasn't a good sign.

Silva placed rubber plugs in the barrels of her weapons before wading the river. The weapons could still dry themselves out and fire when wet, but the women had all picked up the rubber plugs awhile back after they realized—in the middle of a firefight—that it took almost a minute for the weapons to become combat ready after being completely submerged.

Kelly and Rika followed suit, but stayed in the river, while Silva climbed the far shore and the ravine's steep eastern slope. The pair took a moment to splash water over their helmets and scrub their armor as best they could with moss and brush from the banks. After a minute of cleaning, Rika's rad-counter began to tone down, and she felt a lot better knowing that her insides wouldn't liquefy anytime soon.

Her internal bio-systems had already dosed her with a cocktail of chemicals to keep her innards safe, and her nano was scrubbing her blood; but not walking around covered in radioactive dust was still the best way to live a long life.

Once Rika and Kelly satisfied themselves that they were clean, they each pulled a small pouch from their packs. Within each pouch were four bags. Rika and Kelly pushed a button on each bag, which filled with air before their shells solidified. They attached the bags to their arms and legs, and then the bags pumped out all the air, creating near-perfect vacuums. It wasn't enough to lift their 215kg bodies by any means, but it would allow them to float down the river without dragging on the bottom. The pumps would adjust their buoyancy to ensure they remained below the water's surface and out of sight

<It's kinda relaxing,> Kelly commented as they floated downstream.

<Don't fall asleep, there are some big rocks down here,> Rika replied.

Kelly managed to make a snorting sound over the link. *<Eh? What? Sorry, I dozed off there.>*

<Funny.>

Rika wondered how Kelly could joke at a time like this. Just over ten minutes ago, they had watched their entire company get killed by a tacnuke. Sure, most of them were assholes—especially Gunny—but some had treated the mechs with respect. There was a particular staff sergeant named Tony who had always been more than cordial to Rika.

Now Tony was a charred husk left on the battlefield.

Kelly had never made a connection to anyone in the company. She rarely spoke to anyone other than Rika and Silva. It was probably a good thing, since her mouth tended to get her in a lot of trouble when she opened it—metaphorically speaking, of course.

Rika would also miss Lance, the company AI. He wasn't terribly bright, and probably not actually sentient—though the military claimed all their AI were—but he still treated the mechs with respect. Maybe he was in a similar situation. Rika had a suspicion that most of the AI in the military were not there of their own free will. It made no sense otherwise; why would an AI—a being of pure logic and reason with an eternity ahead of them—join a war?

A splash sounded nearby and Silva's voice came to them. <*Hold up a sec, let me wash off and get buoyant.*>

<*Any sign of them?*> Rika asked as she gripped a large rock with her tri-clawed feet.

<*Who, the Nietzscheans, or a signal from battalion HQ?*> Silva asked wearily.

<*Both…I guess,*> Rika replied.

<*Nothing from the battalion. Atmospherics are a mess—that wasn't the only nuke that went off around here. I can't get a signal anywhere,*> Silva said. <*The Niets, on the other hand, are after us like hounds sniffing out a bone. This river bends southeast after awhile, though. It'll take us close to where the battalion had their HQ. We'll see if we can find them, but if not, we'll carry on downstream to Denmar.*>

<*Denmar…*> Kelly murmured. <*Think it's still standing? It's a pretty big city…. I wonder if there are any good med-techs there.*>

<*Stop that line of thought,*> Silva ordered. <*Gunny doesn't need to be around for your Discipline to trigger. It's in there till the military docs take it out. You know what happens to mechs that try to mess with it.*>

<*I just want to—*> Kelly's voice snapped off, and Rika's augmented hearing could hear frantic splashes nearby.

<*Told you,*> Silva said a minute later when Kelly's flailing had ceased. <*Now lock that thinking down. If the Niets had been nearby, we'd all be dead.*>

Rika appreciated Silva's sentiment, even though they knew no Niets were within a klick—thanks to the feeds from their few remaining drones. Rika knew those eyes in the sky wouldn't last much longer; most had burned up when the final tacnuke went off. The five still up there only had another few hours before their batteries would run dry.

Silva must have been on the same train of thought. <*Rika, Kelly, pull your drones down and charge them up. When they're back up, I'll pull mine down.*>

<*My charging sockets are knackered,*> Kelly said, her mental tone wavering in the aftershock of the compliance chip's Discipline. <*Rika, I'll slave mine to you so you can pull 'em.*>

<*You got it,*> Rika replied as control of Kelly's two drones passed to her. She pulled down the miniscule robots, waiting for them to come into

their final approach before stretching her left arm out of the water and registering their insertion into her charging sockets.

<*Ten minutes to charge,*> Rika said to the team. <*Damn, one of mine is on the fritz; it won't take a charge. I'm seeing if it can be repaired.*>

<*Next time we take more drones,*> Kelly groused.

<*And a spare arm?*> Rika asked with a laugh.

<*They may have a spare at the battalion HQ,*> Silva said. <*Weapons too.*>

<*If it's still there,*> Kelly said. <*I bet they just cut and run.*>

<*Or they met a nuke,*> Rika said somberly. <*Though the mech resupply pods are hardened; there may still be something for us to salvage.*>

<*Good call, Rika. Having Kelly fully operational would be a boon,*> Silva replied.

<*A boon?*> Kelly replied. <*What the hell is that? Sounds like a type of monkey.*>

<*Fuck, Kelly, do you like being dumb?*> Rika swore. For some reason Kelly's comment had pushed her over the edge and she didn't know why. The ambush, the K1R, the nukes—it was more than she could even process. Rika considered holding back,

but she was too tired, scared, and angry. *<A boon is the fucking opposite of bane. Bane bad, boon good. And baboons aren't even fucking monkeys, for fucksakes.>*

<Kay, fine…I get it,> Kelly replied, her mental tone more meek than defensive.

The team fell silent after that, other than Rika announcing that her drones—except for the one that wouldn't take a charge—were ready to go. She sent them up into the sky while Silva pulled hers down.

Rika regretted snapping at Kelly, but she didn't know what to say to smooth things over. She was afraid that Kelly was fuming, ready to lash out the moment Rika tried to talk to her. She went around and around in her mind, preparing defenses should the argument occur; worried that Kelly would hate her now, and that she would lose one of the only two friends she had in the whole damn universe.

A part of her knew it was silly. Kelly would be fine—though she *was* capable of holding a grudge for a good while.

Eventually, the river came out of the hill country, widened, and slowed. Rika began to doze off as the languid current carried the three submerged women downstream. She knew it would be another hour until they reached the point where they would leave the water's cover and begin the fifty-kilometer overland trek to the battalion HQ, so she set an alarm to wake her before they arrived.

Rika never fell fully asleep; her combat stims wouldn't let her. But she managed to drift into a peaceful half-doze, which was rudely interrupted by the alarm in her mind that warned of their approach to Silva's designated debarkation point.

<*Have a nice nap?*> Silva asked.

<*Kinda,*> Rika replied cautiously, worried Silva would be upset.

<*I think Kelly's still asleep,*> Silva said with a chuckle. <*I caught a few winks, too. Hard not to, with the river rocking us like babies.*>

<*Hah,*> Kelly snorted. <*I just got the image of little mech babies.*>

<*Sounds like the stuff of nightmares,*> Silva replied.

Rika had to agree. Giving birth to mech babies was a recurring dream she had; one that would have woken her up in a cold sweat, if she could still sweat. At least she could still wake up when she wanted to—most of the time. She had heard that mech-meat, like that poor sap in the K1R, couldn't even control their own sleep cycles.

<*Looks clear out there,*> Rika said, changing the subject.

<*It does…too clear. You'd think there'd be Niets around here somewhere. They* ***are*** *trying to take the planet, last I heard,*> Kelly added.

<*Doesn't matter,*> Silva replied. <*We can't float around all day. Let's go check out the HQ.*>

The three women of team Hammerfall emerged from the river like a trio of mechanized dryads; water sloughing off them, their matte grey armor gleaming in Parson's light before their active camo systems kicked in and they shimmered out of view—except for Rika's thigh, and Kelly's arm, which she cradled against her body to hide from view as much as possible.

<*Too bad we don't have the right kit to just remove that,*> Silva commented, as the stood on the river's shore and looked around at the landscape.

<*I'll manage,*> Kelly replied. <*My armor is torn up almost to the shoulder anyway, and that part doesn't come off.*>

Rika bounded up the low slope at the river's edge to view the plains beyond. The drones overhead had already given her a picture of what lay before them, but she wanted to see it from her own vantage.

The river at the point of their exit was running almost due east, and they stood on the north shore. Stretching for hundreds of kilometers in every direction was a lush plain covered in tall grass, dotted with copses of trees. The beauty was marred by columns of smoke rising from several locations; one corresponding with where the battalion HQ should be.

<Doesn't look promising,> Rika said.

<Still need to go,> Silva replied. *<I haven't been able to link up with the division command, or the fleet either. It's like my comm signals are just going into the ether.>*

They began to move across the prairie, travelling in the open and avoiding the trees, counting on their camo to shield them from prying eyes. The tall grass rose over two meters in some places, and gave enough cover to hide Rika's thigh and Kelly's arm.

Overhead, the drones spotted a Nietzschean patrol to the south, and the women moved north to give it a wide berth. Other than that one sighting, it was as though Naera was devoid of all human life. Rika began to imagine that maybe it was. Maybe both the Nietzscheans and Genevians had left, and they could finally relax.

She allowed herself to indulge in this fantasy for several minutes. Until it was interrupted by a brilliant flash of light on the southern horizon, and the sight of a mushroom cloud rising into the afternoon sky.

<*Seriously, this is getting ridiculou,*> Kelly said with a shake of her head. <*They might as well just nuke this rock from orbit and be done with the whole deal.*>

<*Don't give them any ideas,*> Silva responded.

<*Hey, Kelly,*> Rika said privately. Now was as good a time as any to apologize. <*I'm sorry about how I snapped back there. It was….*>

<*It was nothing,*> Kelly replied too quickly. <*We're all under a lot of pressure, got a lot of shit going on. For you more than me, since you actually liked some of the dickwads in our outfit.*>

<*Seriously, Kelly. I really am sorry. You and Silva are all I have. You're my best friends—Hammerfall is my family. I don't want to lose family.*>

Ahead, Kelly turned her head and Rika imagined that the other woman was smiling.

<It's OK, Rika, seriously. Families fight—it happens—but what we have is thicker than blood. We'll always be team Hammerfall.>

Kelly's mental tone was sincere, and Rika wished she could hug her. A strong need to have some, just a tiny bit, of human contact crashed into her like a towering wave.

Fuck it, she thought, picking up her pace to catch with Kelly. She reached out and touched her teammate on the right shoulder; a gentle stroke, barely perceptible through the layers of armor they wore, but contact.

Kelly shifted as they walked, moving closer to her, and Rika wrapped her arm around Kelly, her mechanical hand resting on the other woman's shoulder. Rika was glad to just feel close to another human—even if it wasn't her real hand that was making contact.

They leaned into one another for a minute, before separating and turning their featureless heads toward each other.

<Thanks,> Kelly said softly. *<That was nice…to feel…like a person.>*

<We're not machines,> Rika replied. *<Even if—>* she paused, forcing her emotions under control. *<Even if we never look human—like women—again, we still are in here.>*

She reached out and tapped Kelly's chest above where she knew their augmented hearts beat, beneath layers of armor and tech. Beneath the mech.

Kelly stopped and her body sagged. *<I need a moment, go on.>*

<No,> Rika replied, and returned to Kelly, wrapping her in an embrace. One vaguely human arm, and one gun mount with a GNR-41B were wrapped around her friend, her sister. They stood like that for several minutes, before they heard a footfall nearby.

Both women snapped out of their reverie and realized that Silva stood a meter from them.

<OK, girls. I could use a good hug right now too, but we have to move. Daylight's wasting, and I want to hit the HQ and be on our way before nightfall.>

<Sorry,> Rika said. *<Sorry I'm not strong enough.>*

<*Shit, Rika,*> Kelly laughed, the sound warbling slightly in their minds. <*You're the strongest woman I've ever seen. You can bitch at me all you want, I won't forget you leaping onto that K1R and saving my life.*>

<*Oh, yeah?*> Silva asked as she beckoned the other two to follow her. <*I didn't hear about that. Sounds like a good story.*>

They took off at a quick trot again as the sun began to set on the western horizon, and Kelly told a rather embellished story of how Rika all but tore the K1R limb from limb to save her.

Eleven minutes later, they approached the coulee where the battalion HQ once lay. They had a pretty good idea of what they were going to see long before they reached it. Their rad-counters had been registering increasing levels for some time, and before they got within five klicks of the camp, they passed into an area where the tall grass had been burned away completely.

The coulee was a shallow depression in the prairie, only forty meters deep in the center, with a small stream winding its way through—or what had once been a small stream. Now it was a slow flow of sludge and ash.

The broken skeletons of trees and transport vehicles were scattered through the coulee with no small number of corpses lying among them.

<*OK, split up,*> Silva said. <*Rika, take the west end of the camp; Kelly, you take the east. I'll work through the center.*>

The women wordlessly split off, and Rika jogged through the ashen terrain to the edge of the coulee above the eastern end of the camp. The slope's incline was gentle here, and she worked her way down, ignoring the bodies she passed.

Most looked like they had been fleeing the camp—she supposed the battalion HQ probably had some advanced warning before they were taken out. Rika wondered how the Niets had fired a tacnuke at the HQ that the air-defense systems didn't detect and shoot down. Maybe it was a high-velocity artillery round, or maybe it was a high altitude drop, or a captured K1R turned rogue…she would probably never know, but it didn't stop her from wondering.

The eastern end of the camp was the motor pool, and she passed a long row of troop transports, several light tanks, and an H82 mech—one that allowed for a regular human pilot. She eyed it, wondering if her SMI-2 body could fit within the massive mech's cocoon. The extra protection would be nice, but it would also make for a dangerously large target out on the prairie.

Stealth was team Hammerfall's most powerful weapon—one that she wasn't going to trade for all the 50mm cannons, tacnukes, and ablative armor in the world.

Just beyond the H82, she spotted a spare cannon for a K1R and a Gatling Gun mount for a J22 model laying on the ground near a toppled stack of crates.

<I found the armory,> Silva called over the link. *<Fully stocked. Looks like we'll get our ordinance up to snuff again.>*

<I found an H82 and some K1R supplies. Going to hunt around and see if there's anything for us here,> Rika added.

<There isn't shit out this way,> Kelly said. *<I'm coming in to you, Silva.>*

<Kay,> Silva replied absently.

Rika looked over the crates, trying to find one that was the right size for SMI-2 parts. Normally she would have scanned the RFIDs, but the nuke had hosed those, and burned off the shipping plas labels as well. She pulled down a few crates that were far too heavy, digging into the stack, then found one that looked right.

She unlatched it and prised the lid off. Bingo!

Inside the case lay a right arm for an SMI-2 mech, plus the toolkit to pull off the old arm and attach the new one. She rifled through several more cases until she finally came upon a fresh set of SMI-2 armor plating.

<Rika's parts store, we deliver,> she called out to Kelly and Silva. *<I just need to find a sled, and I'll be right over.>*

She cast about, knowing that the squishies would need a hover sled to move this equipment. She rounded the crates and saw a smaller case lying on its side. The words "Advanced Field Biological Repair Kit M7.1 – Limbs" were stamped into its metal shell.

Rika wasn't familiar with any Mark 7 repair kits. The one she had used to re-enforce her missing thigh muscle—which still throbbed—was a Mark 5 field kit.

She popped the case open and saw two hollow cylinders. One looked about the right size to fit around her thigh, and the other would encompass an arm. A single card sat in the case and she picked it up. The instructions were simple: they directed the user to clear out any biofoam and other repair tech from the wound, and then slide the cylinder over the limb.

Rika looked down at her leg and frowned. This was probably going to hurt. A lot.

Using her field knife, Rika cut out the biofoam until she got to the re-enforcement rod. She took a deep breath and gave it a twist, unlocking it from its mounts, and carefully pulled it out, whimpering in her mind as the waves of pain tore through her leg and up her body.

She quickly scooped the rest of the biofoam out while she had the nerve. When the crater in her thigh was reasonably clear, she opened the cylinder up into its two halves and then closed it around her thigh.

The pain was instant and excruciating. The only other time Rika had felt anything like it was when her limbs were being sawed off—though somehow this felt even worse. She fought it for a moment, terrified it was simply cutting off the limb, then blessed darkness rolled over her and she knew no more.

*****

<Rika! Rika!>

Something was shaking her, and Rika fought against consciousness as it returned. Couldn't she just sleep in a bit longer?

<Rika! Wake up!>

Rika's vision snapped back on as her augmentations forced her to full awareness. Her right thigh felt like it was on fire, and Rika looked down to see the metal cylinder still wrapped around it. As she tried to focus on what was happening, an indicator on the cylinder flashed green, and then it split into two pieces and fell off.

<Well, shit!> the voice said, and Rika looked up to see both Silva and Kelly standing over her.

<Your leg!> Kelly gestured down at Rika's thigh. *<It's healed.>*

Rika looked down, and saw that Kelly was right. Where there had been a gaping wound exposing muscle and bone, there was now just the smooth matte grey 'skin' all the SMI-2 sported under their armor.

<*Stars…*> she muttered, and ran her hand over her what passed for her flesh. She moved her leg and could feel the muscles beneath bunching and stretching just as they should.

<*You can't flash clone muscle that fast,*> Silva said. <*It must have put in some sort of artificial stuff.*>

<*Great,*> Rika grunted as she stood. <*Just another part of me that's a machine.*>

<*You're the one that decided to clamp the strange metal cylinder around her leg,*> Kelly said with a chuckle. <*It's good, though. You won't be limping along in the back anymore.*>

<*Funny girl,*> Rika said as she picked the smaller cylinder out of the case. <*Your turn.*>

<*Oh, hell no. I saw how your vitals went nuts when that thing did whatever it does. You're not putting it on me. Look, my arm's fine; just a crack in the armor and a tear in the skin,*> Kelly said as she stepped back and waved her ruined arm in protest.

<If there's hardly any damage, then it won't hurt that much,> Silva said. *<We need to be at full operation efficiency if we're gonna make it to Denmar.>*

<Fiiiine, get it over with, then,> Kelly said and held her arm out.

<First let's get this twisted mess off you,> Rika said, and grabbed a tool from the crate containing the new arm. She inserted it into a slot near where Kelly's artificial limb met the mounting socket set into her arm, and gave a solid twist. The tool caught for a second, and then the anchor bolts popped out of Kelly's arm. Rika pulled them out and twisted the cybernetic arm off. She then unlatched Kelly's armor around the shoulder and pulled the plates off, exposing her grey skin underneath.

<Wow, you're pretty good at that,> Kelly commented.

<Hold out your arm,> Rika responded.

Kelly complied, and Rika fitted the cylinder around her stump of a limb, watching as it clamped down and began to hum.

<Motherfucker! Sweet stars, fuck that aaghh fuck!>

<Tell us how you really feel,> Silva chucked.

<*Damn, I never knew you were a sadist,*> Kelly grunted over the Link.

Rika was impressed that Kelly didn't pass out; though the repairs the kit performed on her were far less extensive. Five minutes later, the cylinder came free and Kelly held up her arm, which looked as good as new—well, new for a mech.

Silva attached the new arm to Kelly's socket, and they quickly used pieces from the full armor set that Rika had found for repairs. Ten minutes later, they were ready to get on the move—rearmed, restocked, and eager to get out of the coulee, and away from the corpses filling it.

<*We should stop at the satcomm tower,*> Rika said, pointing at the stubby tower near the center of the camp.

<*It's half melted now,*> Silva said. <*We won't be able to raise anyone on it.*>

<*Yeah,*> Rika nodded. <*But what if it has a stored message, or some sort of intel about where we can get a ride off this rock?*>

<*Smart girl,*> Silva nodded and led the trio to the tower.

The base of the tower was hardened and contained a communications computer, which should have survived the blast. Silva opened the cover and Rika and Kelly shared a glance as the soft glow came from its holoscreen.

<Lets see what's in here,> Silva said as she entered a manual code and pulled up the latest orders.

<Supply…deployments…oh…oh shit…>

<What is it?> Kelly demanded.

<There was some sort of encryption compromise. They switched to a new set of channels and encryption keys—ones we don't have,> Silva said with more than a little worry in her mental tone.

<So they were getting your messages, but ignoring them because you were using compromised encryption?> Kelly asked.

<I guess,> Silva replied. *<Wait, there's one final burst in here…Oh fuck! Oh fuck!>*

<Spill it!> Rika said, more than a little worried about what else could upset Silva so much.

Silva looked up at the other two members of Hammerfall. *<They called for planetary evac…six hours ago.>*

<What's our window?> Rika asked.

<Last dustoff around here is in Denmar, in a little over three hours,> Silva replied as she stood.

<Then what are we waiting for?> Kelly asked.

Silva nodded and kicked the comm unit, smashing the computer inside. *<Hammerfall, let's roll.>*

EVAC

STELLAR DATE: 12.02.8941 (Adjusted Years)
LOCATION: City of Denmar, Naera
REGION: Parson System, Genevian Federation

The three women crouched behind the ruins of a factory on the edges of the city of Denmar. Parson's light was just beginning to fill the eastern sky as they checked their weapons and loadouts for the final push.

They had already fought their way through several platoons of Nietzschean soldiers in their mad dash to reach Denmar on time. However, an entire army of the enemy now lay between them and the evac point.

Rika peered around the edge of the building at the maelstrom of weapons fire that arched between the advancing Nietzscheans and the retreating Genevians.

<*Easy,*> Rika said, her mental tone sounding as tired as she felt. <*Looks like just a hundred-thousand Niets between us and our ships. No biggie.*>

As she finished speaking, a blinding flash of light lit up the buildings around them, far brighter than

Parson's orb shone at high noon, before disappearing and leaving everything looking darker than it had a minute before.

<*Starfire?*> Kelly asked.

Rika checked her rad-counter. It hadn't spiked, so the blast hadn't been an electron or proton beam. An orbital plasma shot was the most likely answer. She peered around the corner again, and saw a stretch of molten ground three hundred yards away.

<*Yup, looks like it. Ours too.*>

<*Nice of fleet to help out for once,*> Silva added. <*Let's not waste their little gift. Get a move on!*>

The three women left the building's cover and dashed across an open stretch of asphalt before ducking behind a row of ground haulers. They kept moving past several more buildings, and then skirted the edge of the area where the ground still glowed from the starfire burst.

Rika wished they still had drones, but their eyes in the sky had been lost when they first engaged the Niets at the edge of Denmar an hour ago. Now they had nothing but their vision to rely on—though with IR and UV overlays, it was still better than what any stock human came equipped with.

<*Contact!*> Kelly called out, and her GNR-41B sniper rifle snicked quietly as it let loose a trio of projectile rounds.

Rika spotted the enemy: a solitary Nietzschean in medium combat armor. The rounds from Kelly's GNR slammed his chest plate; the first two ricocheting off, before the third finally cracked the armor and turned his insides to mush.

<*Nice shot,*> Rika commented.

<*There's more ahead,*> Silva said, and a squad of Nietzschean soldiers lit up on their HUDs, easing along the wall of a half-destroyed building. Lucky for the three women, the enemy was moving in the opposite direction, assuming that nothing had survived the starfire to their rear.

<*Engage or avoid?*> Kelly asked.

<*Let's pass these ones by,*> Silva said. <*We only have forty minutes to make it clear across Denmar, and we can't waste time duking it out with every Nit we see.*>

<*I don't like the idea of an enemy at my back,*> Kelly groused.

<There's a whole Nit army here,> Rika replied. *<If we make too much noise, the enemy's gonna be* ***standing*** *on your back.>*

<Fine,> Kelly sighed as they slipped through the diminishing shadows, moving toward the river.

When they finally reached it, Rika was amazed at how large the river had grown. It was the same water they had slipped into back in the hill country, but now it stretched over a kilometer across. Her HUD gave her spectral analysis, and she saw that the water was much more saline than when they had languidly floated in its currents.

<High tide,> she commented to the team.

<Looks like it. Good for us. Puts the water right up to the embankment ahead,> Silva replied.

Kelly shook her head. *<Too bad there are a thousand Niets between us and it.>*

<Think they'll just let us through if we ask nicely?> Rika asked.

From what they could tell, the far side of the river was still held by Genevians—or at least the amount of weapons fire arching over the water suggested it was. The trio was so close to safety, yet even on their best day—a day when they weren't exhausted and running low on ammunition—they couldn't best a thousand Niets.

<What about drains?> Rika asked. *<They must have storm drains that go into the river.>*

<Good thinking,> Silva said, and ducked back behind a low stone wall toward the closest street. They found several storm drains, each too small, until Kelly called out from the corner of a wide intersection where she stood by a drain slot in the curb.

<Here! We can crack open a party onto this thing to widen the opening up. It looks big enough down below,> she said as Rika and Silva approached.

<Do it,> Silva said.

Kelly twisted a party grenade apart and spilled the thermite packets onto the ground. Then she spread them out across the area she wanted to melt. Once they were arranged to her satisfaction, Kelly manually activated the trigger inside the grenade's shell and the thermite packets flared to life.

"Hey!" a voice called out from down the street. "What are you doing there?"

<Shit, take cover,> Silva ordered and Rika dove behind a car, while Kelly and Silva crouched behind

one of the buildings. Neither the car nor the building offered much cover, but they couldn't go far from the hole they were making if they wanted to get down it before the enemy was on them.

Rika slid her GNR under the car, using its sights to see who had called out. What she spotted was a half-platoon of Niets, all in heavy armor, advancing down the middle of the street. Rika relayed the finding to her team, and then prepared to fire. Her nerves were shot—too much adrenaline and too many bio-stims from her augmentations. She took a deep breath, lined up her weapon, and fired seven bursts in rapid succession.

Four hit, and three tore the feet right off the enemy they struck. The enemy platoon scattered to the edges of the road. With any luck, their newfound caution would buy team Hammerfall enough time for the thermite to do its job.

<Another ten seconds,> Kelly estimated as Silva fired a salvo and then threw a party down the street.

The Niets returned fire, and their armor piercing rounds tore through the car Rika was using for cover. She thanked the stars that penetrating the vehicle slowed the projectiles enough that they bounced off her armor, but at the rate the enemy was firing, there wouldn't be enough of the car left to slow their shots down for long.

<In ten seconds, I'll look like the pavement that thermite is chewing through!> Rika yelled back to Kelly.

<Kay!> Kelly hollered back and burst from behind the building, leapt into the air, and brought all two-hundred-plus kilograms of her body down onto the pavement the thermite was chewing through. With a deafening *SNAP* she disappeared in a massive shower of sparks and fire.

Rika felt guilt stab at her. Had Kelly just killed herself to save them?

<I'm OK!> Kelly called up. *<Half full of water down here—saved me from a rather melty death.>*

<Kelly,> Silva yelled. *<Thermite burns in water!>*

<Oh, shit! It does!>

Rika tried not to smile at the hilarity of their situation as she fired at the vague figures of the Niets where they advanced along the edges of the street. She heard a scream, and then another as her shots found their marks.

Kelly called up again. *<I'm OK, I think.... That's what ablative armor is for, right? To ablate?>*

<So you keep saying,> Rika called back.

<Rika, get down there. I'll cover you,> Silva ordered.

Another round tore through the rapidly disintegrating car and pinged off Rika's armor. She didn't have to be told twice. She scampered across the pavement, diving head first into the hole Kelly had made. She splashed out of the way a second before Silva came down after her.

<Glad you guys could make it,> Kelly said, as she placed a mine on the roof of the tunnel and set it to detonate, five seconds after an enemy passed by.

<Nice place you have here,> Rika replied as she pulled out another mine and placed it ten meters farther down the tunnel, configuring it to detonate the instant Kelly's mine went off.

<Two's good, let's go,> Silva announced as they sloshed through the waist-high water. They'd only made it forty meters when a splash sounded behind them.

<Down!> Rika cried and the three women dove into the water, pulling themselves along the tunnel's floor as shots slapped into the water

around them. Then a concussive shock slammed into their bodies, and a wave of water pushed them forward.

Rika surfaced and looked behind to see that the tunnel had collapsed. She was about to congratulate her teammates when a split formed in the tunnel's ceiling above them.

<*It's coming down!*> Kelly hollered, and the three women surged forward, using all the augmented strength their enhanced muscles and armor offered.

They pushed up over ten kilometers per hour in the tight confines, barely keeping ahead of the collapsing tunnel. Rika was beginning to wonder if the drain dumped right into the river, or if it went to a treatment plant, when she slammed into a metal grate.

Kelly and Silva were there a second later, and the three women pulled at the bars, wrenching them open and escaping just as the tunnel collapsed behind them.

Rika's chest was heaving, desperate to oxygenate her muscles, and working her CO^2 scrubbers overtime. She sank to the bottom of the river, fighting a wave of claustrophobia; her mind trying to remind her body that her armor's systems could keep her going underwater for an hour, if needs be.

Her feet finally hit the riverbed, and her sonar picked up Kelly and Silva hitting the muddy bottom a few meters on either side of her.

<*That was fun,*> Kelly said. <*Let's never do it again.*>

<*Deal,*> Silva replied. <*OK, let's get to the far bank while our side still holds it.*>

It took the three women nearly ten minutes to pull their way through the sucking mud at the bottom of the river, and when they finally heaved themselves onto the shore, they felt like they'd run for a day.

"Don't move!" a man's angry voice called out. "Identify yourselves!"

"Corporal Silva, Alpha Company, 89th battalion, Division 253," Silva said through her armor's speakers. "Any chance we can hitch a ride with you guys?"

"Mechs?" the man, a corporal as well by his insignia, asked as he rose from cover and peered down at them. "You're pretty small for mechs."

"SMI-2's, scout models," Silva replied.

"Better come with me," the man grunted. "Major'll want to know that we have mechs."

The trio of women followed the soldier—a man of medium build in light armor, mismatched at that—through the streets of Denmar, to a squat building sporting a sign which proudly declared, "Denmar Metropolitan Police – Precinct 49"

They walked past a pair of guards in heavy armor who looked them up and down, but didn't speak. Inside, several officers stood around a portable holo projector showing the layout of the city. Rika could see areas highlighted in blue and red. The river divided the two colors, but there were a few places where the red had crossed over to the blue side.

Rika recognized a major, a captain, and two lieutenants.

"What the hell are you?" the major asked as he looked the three women up and down.

"They're the new SMI-2 mechs, sir" the lieutenant to his right offered. "Scout models."

"Scout mechs? I remember hearing something about that. Woulda preferred some K1Rs, but I suppose you three will do. You make it through those Niets on the far side of the river?" the major asked.

"Yes, sir," Silva replied. "Took more than a few of them to their graves while we were at it."

The major looked them over once more, shaking his head at their mud-coated armor and raising an eyebrow at the thermite burns covering Kelly. "I'm sure you did. Looks like you've been through hell. What happened out there, anyway? Yesterday we owned this world; now we're buggering off."

"I don't know, sir," Silva replied. "We got hit hard. A lot of nukes and captured K1Rs took out our company, then our battalion."

"And you survived?" the major asked, his brow arched.

"Sir, mechs don't die. Sir!" Silva gave the standard response the mechs had learned to offer when their superior tactics and survivability made them the last ones standing.

"Let's hope that holds true," The major replied with a shake of his head. "As you can guess, we're not long for this bit of ground. Last birds are ready to take off and we're pulling out. You three meats have the luck of the draw; you're on rearguard."

<*Yes, sir,*> Silva replied and snapped off a salute.

<*For fucksakes can we ever catch a break?*> Kelly asked on their private combat net. <*Now we get to be the mech-meat shield for the squishies?*>

<*Not like it's a new thing,*> Rika replied as the major provided specifics to Silva and sent the three of them out of the building, where they saw several squads of Genevian soldiers rush past.

<*They're pulling back from the river. When the last lines pass us, we fall back along this route,*> Silva said, passing the coordinates to Kelly and Rika. <*No matter what, we make a bird. No heroics. Hammerfall is going home.*>

<*Last one off this rock buys the first round,*> Kelly said, her tone almost jovial.

<*We can't drink,*> Rika replied.

Kelly clasped Rika's shoulder with her robotic hand. <*Some day we will; and on that day, I'll have the tally of who's buying what, don't you worry.*>

<*OK, you two, find some cover. The rest of our squishies are about to fall back past us,*> Silva ordered.

Rika and Kelly complied, and a minute later there was nothing but a few empty streets between them and the oncoming Nietzschean army.

Rika began to worry. They had been through so much, fought so hard, but here they were, staring down the enemy once more. *You're not going to make it off this rock,* a voice said in her head. She forced it away, thankful when Silva gave the order to move.

<Let's not wait to see the whites of their eyes or anything,> Silva said. *<We'll keep right behind our squishies.>*

The three women fell back block by block, covering one another, and taking shots at any Niets they spotted. The going was slow, and they got caught in one brief skirmish, then another. Five minutes later, they were on their own, moving toward the evac point, praying the squishies wouldn't leave without them.

<Girls,> Kelly said as they retreated down a long dark boulevard ten blocks from the evac. *<Why go back with our birds? Why not just let them leave without us, hide for a few days…find someone?>*

<Seriously, Kelly?> Rika asked. *<You pick* ***now*** *to see if you can skirt Discipline?>*

<I just want to get free, Rika,> Kelly pleaded. *<Look at us, we're not warriors. Silva's a waitress who wants to act, I'm a cheap hooker, and you're just some street rat.*

We're not going to survive this war. We're just meat to shield the squishies. I wanna see my kids again!>

Rika's heart went out to Kelly. Rika didn't have anyone…anything at all waiting for her back in the world, other than a good long binge-drinking spree. Kelly had kids. Two girls who were growing up while their mother slogged through the ashes of a dozen ruined worlds.

<*We're a team,*> Rika said. <*Hammerfall takes care of its own. We'll make it through. Fuck, we survived two tacnukes. Now focus.*>

Rika was on the east side of the road, farthest from the enemy they could see furtively working their way up the boulevard a half kilometer distant. She took aim and fired a uranium rod from her GNR, blowing the head clear off a Nit who took too long to get behind cover.

<*She's right, Kelly. C'mon, we're almost clear,*> Silva said from the far side of the road as she turned to look at Kelly, who crouched five meters further down the street. <*When we get back, I'll put in a request to see if you can get a vid of your kids or something.*>

As she spoke, a Nit came around a corner only twenty meters from Silva. Rika could have sworn the side street had been clear, but the enemy must have been well concealed. He was in heavy armor, almost as tall as the SMI-2s, and the weapon he held unleashed a barrage of high-explosive rounds at Silva.

Rika raised her weapon to fire on him, but caught sight of another Nit on her side of the road as he threw a grenade at her. She dove out of the way and scampered behind a car for cover. The grenade rolled under the vehicle and Rika's breath caught as the explosion lifted the vehicle into the air and flung it over her head.

She fought through the shock and rushed her attacker, swinging a fist at his neck, feeling his armor dent. He fell back, trying to bring his weapon to bear, but she swung one of her clawed feet up and snatched the weapon from his hand before planting the other foot on his chest and wrapping it around his torso while grasping the underside of his helmet with her left hand.

Rika heaved up with all her strength, trying to pull the helmet off so she could put one between her attacker's eyes. The man—she thought it was a man, from the build—let loose a terrifyingly unnatural scream as she wrenched the helmet free.

She flung it aside and stepped back, aiming her GNR-41B at his head, ready to pull the trigger…when she realized he was already dead. In her rage, she had pulled his helmet off from the front, tearing his jaw, and much of his face, off in the process.

The scream was still echoing around her, and it took Rika a moment to realize that it was coming from her—all the sorrow, fear, and rage that had been building up inside her, pouring out of her armor's speakers. She wasn't going to lose her family, not today, not at the hands of these assholes. She forced herself to cease the scream—though she wasn't even certain how she did it, and then looked across the boulevard to see Kelly cradling Silva's body

<Is she…> Rika asked as she raced across the boulevard spraying weapons fire down the road, not caring if she hit anything, barely daring to breathe.

<She's alive,> Kelly whispered across the Link. *<Fuck me and my fucking nonsense, I almost got her killed.>*

<Well, no one's dead yet,> Rika said. *<You take her, I'll cover you.>*

As Kelly lifted Silva's limp body, Rika caught sight of a pair of ghastly holes in the corporal's abdomen. Biofoam was spilling out of her armor, staunching the flow of blood and sealing the wounds. Silva's head lolled and Rika thanked the stars that Silva was still conscious.

<Just run, girls,> Silva's voice slipped into their minds. *<Run.>*

Kelly didn't have to be told twice; she took off at top speed. Rika followed, running backwards, firing at everything that looked like an enemy, lobbing parties every hundred meters.

Behind her, Rika's three-sixty vision caught sight of the last troop transport, its ramp still lowered, the last of the squishies rushing into its safe confines.

"Hold the door!" she screamed over her speakers, wishing they had taken the time to get the new Link encryption keys from the major. "Don't you fucking leave without us!"

Against all her fears, the ramp stayed down as Rika and Kelly closed the final hundred meters.

Rika saw Niets flooding in from every direction, and the transport's auto turrets flared in the early morning light, tearing into the enemy, forcing them back.

<*We're gonna make it!*> Rika cried out to Kelly, at the same moment that someone inside the shuttle shrieked: *"INCOMING!"*

Rika saw the missile flash out from amongst the Niets. It was headed straight for her, and she had a moment to examine it and consider that it looked like an eclipsed star, black in the middle with a flaming ring around it.

She broke herself free from the mesmerizing vision in time to dodge out of the way—and see the missile slam squarely into Kelly's back.

The impact flung Kelly forward and Silva slipped from her arms. Both women rolled to a stop on the pavement.

Rika skidded to a halt and dashed back as she heard the transport's thrusters flare to life, its turrets still firing. The sound of weapons and engines faded away as she grabbed Silva and tossed her over her right shoulder before grabbing Kelly by the arm and streaking across the pavement to the transport.

The ramp was half closed and the shuttle was five meters off the ground when Rika used every last bit of energy she had to leap into the air, pulling the limp bodies of team Hammerfall with her. She slammed into the transport's deck hard enough that she could feel the vessel shift under her from the impact.

Rika lowered Silva off her shoulder and set Kelly's body down on the deck—her eyes finally seeing the massive hole torn right through her friend's chest.

Nooooo… Rika moaned in her mind as she collapsed to the deck, faintly hearing one of the squishies whisper, "what the fuck are these things?"

* * * * *

Rika stepped into the mech bay and couldn't help but notice that nearly all the racks were empty. She was the only SMI-2 present, though Silva would join her after she had healed up and debriefed the colonel—probably not in that order.

"Hey, SMI-2-253-89A-3," a young woman called out. "Over here. Let me get you out of that armor."

Rika wondered who the woman was talking to, and then remembered that was *her* serial number. She had spent so much time alone with Hammerfall over the last day, using only first names. She had forgotten that to the military she was just a piece of hardware.

She walked to the woman who gave her a smile. "Rika, is it?"

<Yes,> Rika replied. A tech who bothered to learn the names of the mechs? That was a change.

"I'm Jenn. I heard you guys like to use names; sorry I didn't look it up at first."

<It's OK, we're used to it,> Rika said wearily.

"Yeah, I guess," Jenn replied. "You went through the wringer down there…your armor is pretty much scrap—let's get you out of it so you can relax."

Rika nodded and Jenn helped her out of the layers of ablative plating and nano-carbon mesh until she stood 'naked'. She looked down at her body: fit, lean, grey-skinned—until just before her knees and elbows, where her cyborg limbs began.

"Step back onto the hardmounts," Jenn said, and Rika took a step back, feeling a pair of hooks catch on the two mount points on her back. The hooks lifted her into the air, and the tech grabbed a special tool and slipped it into a cavity above her right leg.

Jenn gave the tool a deft twist, and the leg loosened in its socket. She pulled out the anchor rods, gave the limb a twist, and it came free. She followed the same procedure for Rika's other three limbs, until she hung from the hooks as just a torso and four stubby appendages that ended in meta sockets.

"OK, Rika, let's get this helmet off you," Jenn said as she selected another tool and slid it into a recess under Rika's jaw. She gave the tool a twist, and the featureless oval helmet split in two, exposing Rika's head underneath.

Rika's three-sixty vision snapped off, and she slowly opened her eyes; the only organic part of her visible on the outside. Her vision swam for a minute before she was able to focus on the bay and the tech in front of her.

It was refreshing to finally see another person as just that—a human with skin, hair, clothes, all represented in the proper colors. Not a composite view of optical, IR, and UV, overlaid with threat indicators, bio-analysis, and motion predictors.

Just a human.

Rika bent her head down and looked at her own body—what was left of it. The soft curve of her small breasts, her narrow waist—a bit thicker, with the antimatter bottle tucked inside. She could almost pretend it was soft pink skin—if not for the ports and anchor rod holes dotting her flesh. A tear formed in Rika's eye and slid down her cheek.

"I know," Jenn said, true compassion in her voice as she wiped the tear off Rika's face. "My dad got picked up in a sting and is serving as a mech, too. It was a 'wrong place, wrong time' sort of thing, but I know he's kicking ass for the good guys. What they did to you is brutal, but you're really helping. We're going to win this war, I just know it."

Jenn placed her hand on Rika's chest and gently slid her back into the rack. She carefully hooked up the bio-support tubes and recharge cables to Rika's body before clamping the safety bracket around Rika's waist.

"Wouldn't want you to slam around in there if we hit any bumps," Jenn said with a wink.

Jenn stepped back and grasped the door that would cover her rack and turn it into a tomb. Rika found herself wishing that the tech would leave the door open so that she could *see;* so that she could watch the tech work, so that she could have *some* contact with another human.

She tried to ask for it, but found that her Link had already been shut down in preparation for an enforced sleep and repair cycle.

"Sleep tight, Rika," Jenn said with a smile as she closed the door, and sealed Rika in darkness with her tears and soundless sobs.

THE END

*****

What lies ahead for Rika may be worse than anything she's faced in the past.

If you want to know more, pick up Rika Outcast.

* * * * *

Sign up for the Aeon 14 newsletter and get exclusive stories, information on new releases, news, and info on sales and specials.

www.aeon14.com/signup

THE BOOKS OF AEON 14

Keep up to date with what is releasing in Aeon 14 with the free Aeon 14 Reading Guide.

Origins of Destiny (The Age of Terra)
- Prequel: Storming the Norse Wind
- Book 1: Shore Leave (in Galactic Genesis until Sept 2018)
- Book 2: Operative (Summer 2018)
- Book 3: Blackest Night (Summer 2018)

The Intrepid Saga (The Age of Terra)
- Book 1: Outsystem
- Book 2: A Path in the Darkness
- Book 3: Building Victoria

- The Intrepid Saga Omnibus – *Also contains Destiny Lost, book 1 of the Orion War series*

- Destiny Rising – *Special Author's Extended Edition comprised of both Outsystem and A Path in the Darkness with over 100 pages of new content.*

The Orion War
- Book 1: Destiny Lost
- Book 2: New Canaan
- Book 3: Orion Rising
- Book 4: The Scipio Alliance
- Book 5: Attack on Thebes
- Book 6: War on a Thousand Fronts
- Book 7: Fallen Empire (2018)
- Book 8: Airtha Ascendancy (2018)
- Book 9: The Orion Front (2018)

- Book 10: Starfire (2019)
- Book 11: Race Across Time (2019)
- Book 12: Return to Sol (2019)

Tales of the Orion War
- Book 1: Set the Galaxy on Fire
- Book 2: Ignite the Stars
- Book 3: Burn the Galaxy to Ash (2018)

Perilous Alliance (Age of the Orion War – w/Chris J. Pike)
- Book 1: Close Proximity
- Book 2: Strike Vector
- Book 3: Collision Course
- Book 4: Impact Imminent
- Book 5: Critical Inertia (2018)

Rika's Marauders (Age of the Orion War)
- Prequel: Rika Mechanized
- Book 1: Rika Outcast
- Book 2: Rika Redeemed
- Book 3: Rika Triumphant
- Book 4: Rika Commander
- Book 5: Rika Infiltrator (2018)
- Book 6: Rika Unleashed (2018)
- Book 7: Rika Conqueror (2019)

Perseus Gate (Age of the Orion War)
Season 1: Orion Space
- Episode 1: The Gate at the Grey Wolf Star
- Episode 2: The World at the Edge of Space
- Episode 3: The Dance on the Moons of Serenity
- Episode 4: The Last Bastion of Star City
- Episode 5: The Toll Road Between the Stars
- Episode 6: The Final Stroll on Perseus's Arm

- Eps 1-3 Omnibus: The Trail Through the Stars
- Eps 4-6 Omnibus: The Path Amongst the Clouds

Season 2: Inner Stars
- Episode 1: A Meeting of Bodies and Minds
- Episode 3: A Deception and a Promise Kept
- Episode 3: A Surreptitious Rescue of Friends and Foes (2018)
- Episode 4: A Trial and the Tribulations (2018)
- Episode 5: A Deal and a True Story Told (2018)
- Episode 6: A New Empire and An Old Ally (2018)

Season 3: AI Empire
- Episode 1: Restitution and Recompense (2019)
- Five more episodes following…

The Warlord (Before the Age of the Orion War)
- Book 1: The Woman Without a World
- Book 2: The Woman Who Seized an Empire
- Book 3: The Woman Who Lost Everything

The Sentience Wars: Origins (Age of the Sentience Wars – w/James S. Aaron)
- Book 1: Lyssa's Dream
- Book 2: Lyssa's Run
- Book 3: Lyssa's Flight
- Book 4: Lyssa's Call
- Book 5: Lyssa's Flame (June 2018)

Enfield Genesis (Age of the Sentience Wars – w/Lisa Richman)
- Book 1: Alpha Centauri
- Book 2: Proxima Centauri (2018)

Hand's Assassin (Age of the Orion War – w/T.G. Ayer)
- Book 1: Death Dealer

- Book 2: Death Mark (August 2018)

Machete System Bounty Hunter (Age of the Orion War – w/Zen DiPietro)
- Book 1: Hired Gun
- Book 2: Gunning for Trouble
- Book 3: With Guns Blazing (June 2018)

Vexa Legacy (Age of the FTL Wars – w/Andrew Gates)
- Book 1: Seas of the Red Star

Building New Canaan (Age of the Orion War – w/J.J. Green
- Book 1: Carthage (2018)

Fennington Station Murder Mysteries (Age of the Orion War)
- Book 1: Whole Latte Death (w/Chris J. Pike)
- Book 2: Cocoa Crush (w/Chris J. Pike)

The Empire (Age of the Orion War)
- The Empress and the Ambassador (2018)
- Consort of the Scorpion Empress (2018)
- By the Empress's Command (2018)

The Sol Dissolution (The Age of Terra)
- Book 1: Venusian Uprising (2018)
- Book 2: Scattered Disk (2018)
- Book 3: Jovian Offensive (2019)
- Book 4: Fall of Terra (2019)

ABOUT THE AUTHOR

Michael Cooper likes to think of himself as a jack of all trades (and hopes to become master of a few). When not writing, he can be found writing software, working in his shop at his latest carpentry project, or likely reading a book.

He shares his home with a precocious young girl, his wonderful wife (who also writes), two cats, a never-ending list of things he would like to build, and ideas...

Find out what's coming next at www.aeon14.com

Made in the USA
Middletown, DE
19 August 2021

45369061R00071